Ricky, Rocky, and Ringo
ON TV
by MAURI KUNNAS

Crown Publishers, Inc.   New York

Ricky, Rocky, and Ringo had plans for a very
special day. They were asked to sing a pirate
song on a TV show!

"Welcome, boys," said Sally. "Will this be your
first time on TV?"

"Yes," answered Ricky. "And I don't mind saying
we're just a little bit nervous."

"Don't be worried," Sally said. "I'm here to help
you."

First, Sally took the boys to the costume room.
"You need to look like scary pirates," she said.

"Look, guys, Indians!!" Rocky cried. "Isn't this
  exciting?"
"It sure is," Ricky said. "I hope everything goes well."
"Do you think this pirate hat is too big for me?"
  Ringo asked.

Next, Sally brought the boys to the make-up room.
"Even your mother won't know you," said the make-up girl.
"Please relax, Ricky. It's hard to draw this scar while you're shaking."

"Not that way, Ricky!" Sally called. "Those men are carrying jungle sets to Studio 5."
But Ricky didn't seem to hear. He was mumbling to himself.
"Uh-oh," said Rocky. "Poor Ricky's trying to remember the words to our song."

"Walk quietly, boys," Sally whispered. "They
are taping a Christmas show in this studio."
"I wish I could play a horn," Ricky thought.
"Then I wouldn't need to remember any words."

Soon, Ricky, Rocky, and Ringo arrived at their
studio.
"Welcome, boys. I'm Franny, the director.
Everything is ready for you. There's the pirate
ship, the lights, cameras, and microphones."
"So much stuff for our little song?" Ricky said.
"Oh, don't be afraid. It will be over before you
know it," Franny said.

The boys took their places in front of the cameras.

"I wonder if people will think we're on a real pirate ship." Rocky laughed. "These lights sure are hot!"

"A-a-are they r-r-really?" said Ricky. His teeth chattered and his knees knocked together.

"Look into the camera with the red light," the director called.

"Roll 'em!!!" said Franny. The boys began their
    song, but Ricky jumbled the words right away.
"F-f-fifteen hens on a red man's guest," Ricky
    squeaked. "Yo! Ho! Ho! And a bootle tum tum!"
"Cut!" Franny cried.
"Oh, no!" said Ricky. "I can't remember
    anything!"

"Don't worry, Ricky." Franny laughed. "This happens all the time to even the best performers."

"Really?" Ricky asked.

"Oh, yes!" said Sally. "And we have a simple solution." Sally wrote all the words down on big white sheets of paper. She stood next to the camera where no one but Ricky, Rocky, and Ringo could see her.

The boys had one more big job to do. They wanted all their friends and family to see them on TV.
Ricky gathered his family in the living room.

"Why don't I make some cocoa," Mother said.
"The show won't start for three more hours.
I promise to come back in time."

"Fifteen men on the Dead Man's Chest!
Yo! Ho! Ho! And a bottle of rum!"

The whole town watched three wild pirates
sing a fine pirate song.

When it was over, Grandpa said, "That was wonderful, boys! When I was your age, I was quite a singer too. There was just one problem—I could never remember the words."

Manufactured in Japan

Library of Congress Cataloging-in-Publication Data

Kunnas, Mauri. Ricky, Rocky, and Ringo on TV.
(It's great to read and learn!)
Summary: Ricky, Rocky, and Ringo make a television appearance to sing a pirate song, but Ricky experiences stage fright and can't remember the words. [1. Television – Fiction. 2. Rhinoceros – Fiction]
I. Title. II. Series.
PZ7.K9492Rgc 1986   [E]   85-11512

ISBN 0-517-56414-9
10 9 8 7 6 5 4 3 2 1
First Edition